PRAXUS
OF
LITHONIA

Praxus of Lithonia is a work of fiction. References to real people, events, establishments, organizations, or locales are intended only to provide the sense of authenticity and are use fictitiously. All other characters, all incidents, dialogue are drawn from the author's imagination and are not to be seen as real.

Copyright © 2021. Dark Titan Entertainment.

All rights reserved.

Also available in eBook.

Mark Porter of Argoron and *Raiders of Vanok* are available in paperback and eBook formats.

Published by Dark Titan Publishing. A division of Dark Titan Entertainment.

Prodigious Worlds is an imprint of Dark Titan Entertainment.

Paperback ISBN: 979-8-9851109-1-3
eBook ISBN: 979-8-9851109-2-0

darktitanentertainment.com

WORKS BY TY'RON W. C. ROBINSON II

BOOKS/SHORT STORIES

DARK TITAN UNIVERSE SAGA

MAIN SERIES
Dark Titan Knights
The Resistance Protocol
Tales of the Scattered
Tales of the Numinous
Day of Octagon
Crossbreed
Heaven's Called
The Oranos Imperative

Forthcoming
Underworld
Magicks and Mysticism
The Resistance vs. The Enforcement Order

SPIN-OFFS
In A Glass of Dawn: The Casebook of Travis Vail
Maveth: Bloodsport
The Curse of The Mutant-Thing

Forthcoming
Trail of Vengeance
War of The Thunder Gods
Maveth vs. The Swordman

ONE-SHOTS
Maveth, The Death-Bringer
Mystery of The Mutant-Thing
Shade & Switchblade
Retribution of Cain
The Mythologists
Ambush Bot
Kang-Zhu

COLLECTIONS
Dark Titan Omnibus: Volume 1
Dark Titan Omnibus: Volume 2
Dark Titan One-Shot Collection

THE HAUNTED CITY SAGA
The Legendary Warslinger: The Haunted City I
Battle of Astolat: A Haunted City Prequel (KOBO Exclusive)
Redemption of the Lost: The Haunted City II
Consequences of the Suffering: The Haunted City III (Forthcoming)

SYMBOLUM VENATORES
Symbolum Venatores: The Gabriel Kane Collection
Hod: A Symbolum Venatores Book
Symbolum Venatores: War of The Two Kingdoms
Symbolum Venatores: Elrad's Chronicles
Symbolum Venatores: Mystery of the Magician (Forthcoming)
Symbolum Venatores: Twilight of the Gods (Forthcoming)

EVERWAR UNIVERSE
EverWar Universe: Knights & Lords
EverWar Universe: The Damned Ones (Forthcoming)

PRODIGIOUS WORLDS
Mark Porter of Argoron
Raiders of Vanok
Praxus of Lithonia (Forthcoming)

FRIGHTENED! SERIES
Frightened!: The Beginning
Frightened!: The Light Sky (Forthcoming)

INSTINCTS SERIES
Lost in Shadows: Remastered
Instincts: Point Hope (Forthcoming)
Shadow in the Mirror: Instincts II (Forthcoming)

CHEVAH MYTHOS
The Eleventh Hour; A Chevah Mythos Story

THE HORDE TRILOGY
The Horde
The Dreaded Ones (Forthcoming)
Our Sealed Fate (Forthcoming)

DARK TITAN'S THE DEAD DAYS
Accounts of The Dead Days
Brand New Day: The Dead Days I (Forthcoming)

OTHER BOOKS
The Book of The Elect
The Extended Age Omnibus
The Supreme Pursuer: Darkness of the Hunt and Other Stories
Massacre in the Dusk (Forthcoming)

THE DARK TITAN AUDIO EXPERIENCE PODCAST
Season 1: Introductions
Season 2: In a Glass of Dawn
Season 2.5: Accounts of The Dead Days
Season 3: Battle For Astolat
Season 4: Hallow Sword: Cursed

PRAXUS OF LITHONIA

TY'RON W. C. ROBINSON II

CONTENTS

PRAXUS OF LITHONIA
- CHAPTER 1 - 1
- CHAPTER 2 - 4
- CHAPTER 3 - 7
- CHAPTER 4 - 15
- CHAPTER 5 - 23

MARK PORTER OF ARGORON EXCERPTS
- CHAPTER 1: THE INCIDENT - 28
- CHAPTER 2: CAPTIVE FOREIGNER - 32
- CHAPTER 3: WHO ARE YOU? - 38

RAIDERS OF VANOK EXCERPTS
- CHAPTER 1: VANCE HARLAN - 42
- CHAPTER 2: WELCOME ABOARD - 48
- CHAPTER 3: CALYPSO - 53

CHAPTER I

In the early years, there was a kingdom.

A kingdom known as Bandoria.

Bandoria was a kingdom of great wealth and power as was its ruler, King Bantos. Many who had lived in Bandoria were truly successful in their lives, both personally and financially. Even though the rich had lived in Bandoria, there was another kingdom on the outskirts. A kingdom much smaller than the glory of Bandoria's towers and high walls. A kingdom which held a great many people. This kingdom is Lithonia. Lithonia was the sister kingdom to Bandoria, but did not share the rich and powerful delicacies of Bandoria's stature. Majority of the poor had dwelled in the walls of Lithonia, only due to the fact of not being allowed through the walls and onto the grounds of Bandoria.

One day, King Bantos had stepped out and gazed over the balcony of his palace. Looking out toward all the kingdom in its glory. As far out as his eye could wander. Glaring ahead, Bantos caught the glimmering light outside of the kingdom walls. He knew the light had sparked from Lithonia and his anger was quenched.

"This is my kingdom and these lands will belong to me." Bantos said toward his Vizier who stood beside him.

"My lord, what are your plans in overtaking the Lithonians from their kingdom? What of their king? What of their warriors?"

"We have hundreds of warriors prepped for battle, do we not?"

"Yes, my lord. Yes we do."

"Then we need not worry. That dirt-filled place they call a kingdom will be ours soon enough."

During these early years of the war between Bandoria and Lithonia, there was a great falling of many warriors on both sides. In another place within the boundaries of Lithonia, there was a woman who was known as Arinia who had given birth to a son. Her husband, Krotax, a warrior in the clan of Lithonians proclaimed his son's name as Praxus. A Lithonian name and in the Lithonian tongue meant *"ruler and conqueror"*. through the wars, they lived a happy life, even in the times of hardship and trouble from the Bandorian forces. They watched their son grow older through the conflicts.

Praxus himself in his youth became helpful to those in need as he watched Bandorian warriors invade their homes and slaughter the innocent. In one altercation, Praxus took it upon himself and slew two Bandorian warriors with his bare hands, proving to those who witnessed and his mother and father he possessed near superhuman strength. Once he became an adult, he volunteered in the battle against Bantos' forces and witnessed the death of his mother and father by Bantos' own hand. That day was the defeat of Lithnoia and it had fully become under the control of Bandoria.

Ever since their deaths, Praxus went into hiding in the undergrounds of Lithonia. Places Bantos and his advisors had possessed no knowledge of their existence. Gathering other mighty men and women of valor who saw Praxus' strength in times past. They came together and sought to overthrow Bantos and take by Lithonia for the people and to free the bonds of Bandoria from any other lands they may have conquered. Praxus made a vow to avenge the deaths of his people and his mother and father by killing Bantos himself and conquering Bandoria for the taking.

It all begins this day.

CHAPTER II

Now, Praxus and his small army of warriors had made their journey eastward, toward the Kingdom of Brithrow. A providence of Bandoria.

"What are we looking for, Praxus?" a soldier asked.

"Anything that could lead us to King Bantos." Praxus said.

"Then, why are we heading towards the Kingdom of Brithrow? I'm not sure on what you have planned."

"When we enter the gates of Brithrow, you'll see what my plans comes into being."

Riding along through the valleys, they come to a stop and find themselves facing the gates of the Kingdom of Brithrow. Standing by the gates are the Brithrowian Knights, dressed in their iron-clad armor and helmets. Their stained swords held in their hands and pressed against their chests. Their eyes are solely focused on Praxus and those of the Lithionian army. One knight made his way toward Praxus. Walking calmly, yet nervous.

"Might I ask why you have decided to come?"

"I've come to speak with your king." Praxus answered. "He and I are on good terms with one another and I would be pleased to speak to him."

The knight nodded and waved his right hand, signaling the knights to open the gates of the kingdom. The knights slowly open the gates as Praxus and his army enter into the kingdom.

The residents of the kingdom look and see Praxus and his army coming through the kingdom, their horses moving with pace as they approached the castle of Brithrow's king, King Brithon. From the castle doors, walked out Brithon. His gaze looked around as he could hear the sounds of the horses and immediately turned to see Praxus and his army coming toward him.

"My, my. We have visitors." Brithon said.

Praxus' horse stopped in front of the castle. He looked at Brithon, whose standing at the doorway. Praxus gets off his horse and walked up the stony steps to approach Brithon. Brithon made his way to greet Praxus and they greet one another. As if they are close friends.

"Praxus of Lithonia has come to visit me."

"It is for an urgent matter."

"Come inside. We can talk there."

Praxus and Brithon enter into the castle walls as the Brithrow servants take Praxus' horse and his army's horses to their staples to rest up. The army followed the servants to the inside of the castle where they would be fed. Inside the castle, Praxus and Brithon talked about the current situations across the lands. Brithon already knows of the reasons for Praxus' rise in appearances ad why he's come to his kingdom on a short notice.

"I know why you've come here."

"Then you are aware that this is no time for any games to be played."

"I know you want to see King Bantos and his reign come to an end."

"I want his head impaled onto the tip of my sword."

"I figured as much. Which is why I have an offer for you concerning these dire matters."

"What is the offer you proposed?"

"That you aid me in your assistance against Bantos and his

army. Granted, you know this Battle of Kings cannot last much longer."

Praxus thought to himself, detailing the proposal and what it would allow him to do, to get into Bandor and kill Bantos himself to avenge his parents' deaths. He nodded, facing Brithon. Praxus extended his arm in agreement.

"I shall assist you in this battle."

"Wonderful! When they see the two of us on the battlefield facing them, only fear will grab them by their throats and feed them to us."

"I do have one condition regarding this agreement of ours."

"Tell me."

"When we find Bantos, leave him to me."

Brithon nodded with a smile on face. He enjoys seeing the savagery coming through Praxus' words. He knew that he would be the right man to tag along with when it comes to war. Brithon extended his arm and the two came to an agreement. The deal was finalized.

"Agreed."

Praxus and his army remained within the Kingdom of Brithrow for the remainder of the day and spend the night within the kingdom. During those hours, Praxus and Brithon spoke to each other concerning the art of war and the use of weapons in the warfare. Praxus' army feasted and even laid with women that night. Praxus, on the other hand continue to have conversations with Brithon and they later went their separate ways to rest for the mission ahead.

CHAPTER III

The sun had risen and from the castle doors walked out Praxus and his army. They were prepared for the battle ahead. Brithon had approached Praxus from behind and patted him on his back. The two armies were easily to be told apart. Praxus' army dressed in simple garb. Loincloths of leather and fur with armbands and leather-padded boots. Some carried swords as the others wielded bows and arrows. Brithon's army were like a pack of wolves moving in a single-file line. Horned helmets and glistening armor. Swords bulging from their sides and arrows sharp on their backs.

"I surely hope that we can finish Bandor's army off before we come into conflict with him."

"Trust me, we will get through his army. They won't stand a chance."

Praxus and his army get atop their horses and gallop with Brithon and his army following them as they exit his kingdom. While they rode off, Praxus knew that Bantos was in his sights and he wouldn't let anyone or anything get in his way. Brithon's horse managed to catch up to Praxus.

"When we reach Bantos and his army, Praxus, I want you to know that whatever happens, happens."

"That's fair."

"I know for a fact that Bantos will indeed be present on the battlefield. But, he may have brought himself some form of assistance."

"What kind of assistance would he have?"

"We'll know once we get there."

"I understand."

Riding closer toward the field, in the distance one of Praxus' solders managed to catch a glimpse at the soaring army of Bantos. Pointing ahead, they each stare toward the field and see the soldiers moving in succession with the faint sound of chanting echoing through the air across the mountains of the valley. Praxus stopped and rallied his army to cease their movements. Brithon seeing this had done the same.

"What are they saying?" Praxus asked.

"I can't make it out. I know it's a war cry."

"Hmm. They know we're here. I can see that. Where's Bantos? Can you see him through the mess that is his army?"

Brithon took a gander toward the field in which was before them. The field itself laid near the Bandorian Jungle. A place filled with dwelling creatures of immense size. Although, no sign of the ravenous beasts were seen, Brithon believed Bantos had managed to keep them at bay for the battle ahead. Still looking, Brithon spotted one horsemen suited in armor from his head to his feet. An armor unlike the leather and metal pads which the other soldiers wore. With a single nod, Praxus knew the answer and rode down the valley toward the field as his army followed.

The armies moved with haste to reach the field as Bantos himself saw their arrival. His soldiers chanting had went still. Their hands attached to their swords and spears as Bantos rode forward to meet the opposing armies. Their numbers did not bother the Bandorian king, only amused him for a day of slaughter. Praxus and Brithon reached the field, stopping mere feet in front of Bantos and his army. Praxus' eyes seared with anger and Brithon knew it, waving his hands for Praxus to control himself.

"I am amused and yet surprised you managed to accept this battle." Bantos chuckled. "You even brought yourself some reinforcements. Only goes to show you knew this day would be your last."

"I don't think this day is my end." Brithon replied. "You see, my backup came to me to confront you themselves. Their leader, Praxus seeks to bring a better world for his people."

"His people? And who are his people?"

"Lithonians." Praxus answered boldly. "You massacred many of them during your conflicts of conquest."

"I did what a king would have done. I simply conquered lands suited for the better."

"And killing innocent men, women, and children was part of your conquest? The soldiers weren't enough? The warriors weren't proven enough?"

"Praxus, control yourself." Brithon whispered.

Bantos took a look toward Praxus. His eyes keen as he rubbed his chin.

"Have I done something to you in the past, boy?"

"You've done enough."

"Afraid I haven't. I won't be finished until all kingdoms belong to me. Your friend, Brithon's kingdom is just the next one on my list. Damn Brithrowians nor a pair of savage Lithonians will stop me from my conquest."

Praxus took out his sword, holding it high as his army follows. Dozens of swords for Bantos and his army to see. A grin grew on the face of the Bandorian king as he shouted for his soldiers to attack. The armies went and clashed their blades one o another. Bantos did not flee the battleground as some leaders in times past. This king was deep into the fight, slaughtering Brithrowians and Lithonians with ease. Even for someone of his older age. Praxus moved swiftly through the battlefield, taking out Bandorian soldiers like practice. Their heads slicing off their bodies and falling into the bloody grass. Praxus huffed as he moved with haste toward Bantos.

Over next to where Praxus walked, Brithon fought alongside his soldiers and the Lithonian warriors. The fight became bloodier as the minutes had passed. Praxus sliced his way closer to Bantos as he saw him take out three Lithonians with one blow. An impressive feat even in Praxus' eyes. With the three bodies falling to the ground, Bantos looked up and saw Praxus standing before him. Fire in his eyes. Anger boiling beyond its point.

"I did something to you, didn't I?" Bantos asked.

"You took my mother and father from this life. Robbed me of my heritage."

"Did I? Well, get in line with the others who have said the same and die for their honor."

"The only one dying today is you and your rule!"

"Make it so, savage!'

Praxus with anger in his forefront rushed toward Bantos, swiping his sword against Bantos' own. The two stepped back in the midst of the dying screams and flying sprays of blood across the field. Bantos relished in the moment while Praxus continued to let his anger control him. Stepping with speed and haste, Praxus slammed his sword against Bantos as the Bandorian king deflected the blows and kicked the knee of Praxus, knocking him back before Bantos delivered an elbow swipe to the Lithonian's forehead.

"Your anger. It's getting the better of you. Better get it in place, boy, before you end up killing yourself."

"Enough of your damn talking! Fight me!"

Praxus immediately rose to his feet, his sword in hand facing forward as he stretched out toward Bantos and ended up tapping his sword against Bantos' own. A chuckle echoed from the mouth of the Bandorian king as he shoved Praxus back. A grunt of anger busted from the Lithonia as he went for another strike toward Bantos. The king ducked, only for Praxus to be taken down by a heavy blow. A blow which originated from a war hammer. Bantos nodded with a grin as he looked forward, seeing the wielder of the hammer. A towering figure who stood over the height of three Bandorian soldiers. The hammer itself had to have weighed nearly as one of the Bandorian soldiers.

"Figured you would be here."

"I would do anything for you, my king."

The sound of the battle continued on as Bantos knelt down, checking Praxus' pulse. The Lithonian lives. Bandos sighed as he stood up and sheathed his blade. The hammer wielder looked down at Praxus and raised the hammer.

"Do you wish me to end him?"

"Don't." Bantos said. "No need in killing the boy. Death is too sweet for him to savor. Living will do the job."

Lowering the hammer, the wielder and Bantos looked out toward the ongoing remains of the battle. Allowing the wielder to enter the fight, he moved and quickly decimated the Lithonians and Brithowians with ease. Their combined efforts could not match the strength of the wielder and his hammer. Within minutes of the fight, Bantos' army had appeared to have won. Seeing the dead bodies of Lithonians and Brithowians on the ground covered in blood. Some without their heads or insides. Bantos saw the day as a victory and rallied his remaining soldiers to return to Bandoria.

Upon their leave, Brithon arose from a pile of bodies with several living soldiers of his own and a few Lithonians who managed to survive.

"Where's Praxus?" Brithon asked. "Where is he?"

Moving through the bodies, they searched the fields for Praxus and were seemly unable to find him. It was as if he vanished from the battlefield without notice. Knowing Praxus is the kind of warrior who would survive the utmost impossible odds, Brithon in his tired state gathered his soldiers and the Lithonians as they agreed to return to his kingdom in hopes of sending out a unit to find Praxus.

    Deep in the night, hours after the battle. Praxus awoke and found himself inside of a cave. A cave he was unfamiliar with. In front of him, a fire bellowed. A fire he did not conjure nor make. Attempting to stand on his feet, his back pulsed with pain as he dropped to his knees.
    "Do not make a move." said a voice from the darkness of the cave.
    "Who's there?" Praxus questioned. "Step into the light and show yourself."
    "Is that what you crave?"
    "Tell me who you are and why am I here?"
    "Very well, Lithonian."
    The voice moved from the darkness and into the light. Revealing himself to Praxus. A cloaked being dressed in a violet garb. Yet, like a shadow in his movements. His face unseen, yet a mystic power flowed from his very being. He approached the fire and knelt down in front of it. Siphoning some of the flames into his hands. Transferring the energy of the heat into himself.
    "You're a sorcerer." Praxus said.
    "Good of you to notice."
    "I was taught to abhor those like you. Sorcerers are evil and have only done evil to suit their deeds."
    "Such is true for many. Such am I. yet; I will not do the deed of evil this night. For it is not the time."
    Praxus sat up and leaned against the cavern walls. Pressing his back against the rocky walls.

"What are you saying?"

"We were destined to meet this night. It was written thousands of years ago and now, it has come to pass."

"Who are you?"

"I am known as Dakin Maul. A sorcerer who desires this world to be in the hands of my kind."

"I've never heard of you."

"You have now. It is destined for us to be mortal enemies. A man of your barbaric stature could only be a perfect match for a sorcerer like myself. A battle for the ages."

"Then, how come you didn't kill me? Why pull me from the battlefield and bring me here?"

"Because it was not your time to die. Not yet."

"So, was it you who hit me?"

"No. that was Roht. A massive warrior who works under the rulership of King Bantos. He's the one who knocked you unconscious and he sought to kill you, but Bantos spared you. Yet, I already knew of this before it happened."

"Enough of this sorcery talk. Why am I here?"

"To heal. You must return to Brithon to reveal your safe and alive."

"I want Bantos. Where is he?"

"He returned to his kingdom as he should. Don't worry yourself, you'll have your moment with him very soon."

"Answer this for me. Since you know the future, tell me. Do I kill Bantos?"

"Yes," Dakin said with a calm voice.

"Do I kill him soon?"

"I will not say. Just know you indeed kill him and save the kingdoms from the tyrant. When you kill him, I will not reveal."

Praxus leaned his head back and pondered on the thoughts. Dakin knew he was pondering as he showed a faint smirk on his face as it could be seen due to the kindling fire beneath him.

"I need to get going."

"You will remain here for the night. Let your body heal and by the morning light, you shall arise and make your way to Brithon continue your journey."

"And where will you be?"

"I'll be around. It is my destiny to observe you. To learn your skill set for our coming battle. A battle of might versus magic."

"I'll be looking forward to it." Praxus said coldly.

Dakin let out an echoing laugh to Praxus' distaste. A laughter one would deem sinister. A cunning laughter.

"I'm sure you will. As for right now, it is best you sleep."

Dakin reached over and tapped his finger on Praxus' forehead, placing him into a deep sleep.

"We will meet again." Dakin said as he moved back into the darkness of the cave.

CHAPTER IV

The next morning had arisen and Praxus had awoken. Immediately rising to his feet to find Dakin Maul. Hearing no sound within the cave and the fire which was before him had become a shallow pile of burnt wood. The peeking light of the sun touched Praxus' face as he grabbed his sword that was placed against the cavern walls and made his way out. Upon returning to the outside, Praxus stared out into the field of decayed bodies. The remains of the soldiers from the battle before. Their flesh being ripped and torn apart by the Bandorian birds. Feathers as dark as the night. Talons as large as a warrior's boot and beaks sharper than the metal one warrior could wield. There were three of them in the field, yet unaware of Praxus' movements as he stealthy moved past them to avoid a great conflict. One which might bring forth his death if Dakin's words were false.

Praxus took several more steps before he reached the other end of the field. Taking the final step, he pressed into the ground as he paused. His quick pause had slid the dirt under his boot, alerting one of the massive birds. The bird walked toward Praxus as the Lithonia raised up his sword and pointed it toward the creature. The two locked eyes as the bird measured Praxus. In such a close range, the bird stood nearly six feet higher than Praxus. Taking in his scent. Praxus waited for the right moment to strike and the bird raised up its head and let out a small cough before turning away and returning to the dead bodies. Praxus sighed and sheathed his sword, turning away to leave the fields.

Sometime later, King Brithon rested in his castle back in Brithrow. His men moving back and forth from the doors, giving their king details on the remains of his soldiers and the whereabouts of Praxus. Brithon had hoped Praxus indeed survived the battle as he knew the savage Lithonian had the potential to tear down Bantos' tyrannical rule. As one of the soldiers entered the castle, he came with a sense of urgency. Brithon arose from his seat and faced his soldier. He knew what was to come as he stepped forward and walked outside. Looking ahead toward the kingdom's gates, he saw a horse galloping toward him. The rider as he could tell had come from the field. The closer the rider came, the more he knew. A few more inches the rider rode forward and Brithon showed a smile. A smile of relief and hope.

"He's alive."

Praxus stepped from the horse and greeted Brithon and the soldiers who gathered around. Looking at the soldiers, Praxus even saw some of the Lithonian warriors who stood by his side remaining and they saluted one another as brothers-in-arms. With their greetings, Brithon allowed Praxus into the castle to rest up as he could see the tiredness in his eyes, yet his body was full of energy. Entering the king's throne room, the handmaidens had brought the two men wine to drink. Praxus gulped down the drink within seconds and asked for more to the king's pleasure.

"It is good you survived." Brithon said. "Tell me what happened."

"It was simple. I confronted Bantos on the field. Fought him. I believe I had him defeated until I was struck by a heavy blow."

"Struck by who?"

"A warrior called Roht. I was told he was Bantos' right-hand soldier in his rule."

"Who told you this?"

"A sorcerer who aided me without my knowing. A strange fellow. Called himself Dakin Maul."

"Dakin Maul. That's a name I haven't heard in ages. He's still here and around our region."

"I don't know. When I awoke inside the cave, he was gone. Nowhere to be found."

Brithon sighed as he took a sip of the wine, leaning back in his chair.

"Dakin Maul saved you. That's something I've not known him to do. He must have favor in you."

"Said it wasn't my time to die. That he and I have a battle in the future between my strength and his magic."

"Ah. His prophecies speak once more. He's always been the prophetic kind. Telling those of their futures, only for them to come to pass in a way they did not expect."

"So, he was telling the truth? About our battle to come and that I will kill Bantos?"

"What Dakin Maul speaks is the truth in unrighteousness. Only time will unveil what truth will come of it."

Praxus drank more of the wine. Brithon hesitated to tell him to slow down and avoid becoming drunk in his presence. Praxus respected the king's word and took his time. After a while, Brithon informed Praxus of Bantos' return to Bandoria and how he's seeking to rally more soldiers from other lands to take Brithrow from his hands. Praxus lets out his word that he will kill Bantos and he will not wait years to accomplish the goal. Preparing himself to ride out before nightfall that he would arrive in Bandoria to confront Bantos and kill him before the morning broke. Brithon understood Praxus' motivations and agreed with him.

"What do you need me to do?" Brithon asked.

"I cannot allow you to lead yourself and your men into more danger. Bandoria is full of killers who only slaughter for pleasure. I can sneak in alone and deal with whatever forces come my way."

"You can. Meanwhile, myself and a few soldiers of mine will keep the others busy. To give you time to reach Bantos. I heard he speaks a frequent amount of time in his throne room."

Praxus grinned and nodded, extended his arm toward Brithon.

"Then, it's settled."

The two men agreed to the plan and began making moves. Praxus walked outside and gazed upon the sky, seeing the sun reaching west, he left for Bandoria as Brithon and ten of his soldiers each rode out behind Praxus.

Riding out toward the gates of Bandoria by nightfall, Praxus' anger began to bellow within. Brithon looked ahead and saw the guards standing at the gates. He knew if they could take them out, it would give Praxus a better appointee of entering. Praxus agreed to the plan as he made his way toward the gates, sneaking past them by swimming in the moat around. Brithon and his soldiers approached the two guards at the gated entrance.

"Stop. Identity yourselves."

"We come from Brithrow to deliver news to your beloved King Bantos." Brithon spoke.

"And who might you be?"

"The King of Brithrow."

The soldiers paused themselves as their hands dropped down to their swords. Behind them, Praxus arose from the water as his sword moved through the cool air and slashed greatly with his blade, decapitating the soldiers with ease. Impressing even Brithon and his soldiers.

"You move quick."

"We have no choice." Praxus answered. "Otherwise, we'll all be dead."

The soldiers moved to the gate, opening it for Praxus and themselves to enter. The gate opened with a gentle ease as they looked ahead, seeing the city streets clear of civilians and soldiers. Praxus' eyes looked forward toward the massive palace in the distance. He knew Bantos was there and within.

"I'm going for it."

"Be careful, Lithonian." Brithon said. "We'll handle things out here in case it escalates."

Praxus moved through the city, passing by sleeping soldiers and drunken men who relished in the sight of the whores around them. Bantos saw them as a way of keeping the people under his control and he was right. Praxus knew it to be true, seeing the people had no sign of life within their eyes. Their bodies were living , but their souls were drained. Only the faintest sign and taste of pleasure could keep them at bay. No chance of fighting back against Bantos' power. Looking up toward the steps to reach the palace, Praxus ran forward. Nearly thirty steps he reached without fail.

Standing foot on the palace grounds, he moved quietly to avoid the soldiers who patrolled the area. Using the banners and curtains as his way of moving and hiding, Praxus could hear the soldiers talking amongst themselves. Speaking of the battle prior and hw they wished they kill Brithon and took Brithrow for themselves. Continuing his move deeper into the palace as Brithon and the soldiers inched closer to the palace grounds, Praxus moved as he heard the swift sound of a swinging hammer. Hiding behind the wall, he peeked through the curtain and saw Roht standing in the center of the interior garden to the palace.

"You can quit your hiding, Lithonian." Roht spoke. "My king informed me of your arrival would be soon enough."

Praxus stepped from the wall and walked out through the curtain, facing off against Roht. Seeing him in full. A tall brute. His hammer much larger than his sword. Roht scoffed at the sight of Praxus.

"I could've killed you on the field, yet, my king told me not to."

"His foolish decision and his downfall." Praxus said. "All by his own words."

"I think not. This night it will be you falling before his feet after I pummel you with my hammer. The same hammer which knocked you down before."

"What happened before was a cheap blow. This time, I see clearly. Bantos was my only target this night. However, because of your sneak blow, I'll kill you as well."

"Come then." Roht slammed the hammer. "Give your best blow."

Praxus roared, running toward Roht with his sword swinging. Roht deflected the metal with his hammer and kicked Praxus in the abdomen, striking him once more with the top of the hammer, causing him to tremble and fall to the marbled floor. Roht laughed, backing away for Praxus to stand up.

"I will not kill a Lithonian while he's on his back. Stand up and face me once more!"

Praxus gripped his sword and showed a smirk, running toward Roht once more as the brute swung the hammer. Praxus saw the coming attack and slid under the weapon, slashing the left leg of Roht with this sword. The pain shot through his lower body as Praxus elbowed Roht in the chest and kicked him in his abdomen. To his dismay, Roht's flesh felt a similar toughness to a bull. Roht stumbled in his steps, yet maintained his balance.

"Should've worn more armor." Praxus said. "Leaving yourselves bare only give you a weakness."

"Yet, you're barely covered in metal."

"I don't need metal to survive. I'm a Lithonian. All we need is leather, furs, and steel."

Roht raised the hammer above Praxus and went for a pummeling slam. Praxus moved from the hammer's path and threw his sword toward Roht. Straightforward, the blade pierced Roht in his chest. Roht looked at the sword in his chest and pulled it out as the blood oozed from the wound. Throwing the sword to the ground, Roht dropped his hammer and cracked his knuckles.

"Fair play." Praxus said, balling up his fists and stomping his feet.

The two swipe attacks onto one another. Praxus delivering several punches to the face of Roht as the brute snatched Praxus by his hair and dragged him across the garden. Taking his head and shoving it into the dirt of the field. Praxus kicked Roht in the wound of his leg and gasped for air as he rose up from the dirt. Praxus grabbed Roht by his beard and returned the favor, holding his head into the dirt before stomping on the back of his head. Roht rose up, shoving Praxus back as he wiped the dirt from his face and spit onto Praxus' chest. A complete show of disrespect to his own humor. Blood pouring from them both. They clashed once again with punches to the face and kicks to the legs. The sound echoed resembled two beasts clashing in the fields. Praxus slowed down to Roht's pleasure and uppercutted the Lithonian to the ground. Praxus took the moment to catch his breath as he heard the laughter coming from Roht.

"They said Lithonians were savages. Bred for battle. Yet, I look at you and wonder if such a tale is true."

Praxus flipped onto his feet and stared Roht in the eyes with a grin.

"The tales are true. I'm their living embodiment."

Praxus leaped onto Roht and pummeled his face, bringing the brute to his knees. Praxus roared as he kicked Roht in the head, causing him to fall to the floor. Praxus paused and looked down at Roht, seeing he's still breathing. Praxus turned away, looking towards the throne room ahead.

"Where are you going?" Roht said coughing. "You'll have to kill me before you face my king."

"I'm here for him. Not you."

"Either way. You die or we all die."

Praxus looked around and retrieved his sword, sheathing it. Roht screamed continually for Praxus to kill him. Praxus went for his sword and paused. Leaving it be. Instead, he turned to the floor and saw Roht's hammer and lifted the massive weapon to Roht's surprise.

"You cannot be that strong. There is no way."

"Yet, you see it before your very eyes. Your time above this ground is finished. Now, go to your gods. Whomever they be."

Praxus raised the hammer and slammed it atop Roht's head to the sound of a cracking whip. A moment of silence moved through the garden as Praxus looked toward his hands and released the hammer from his hands and turned toward the throne room. Walking slowly as he wiped the blood from his face.

CHAPTER V

Praxus took his steps toward the entrance to the throne room. Hearing the beating sound of distant drums and the flowing sensation of water, Praxus looked around him as he saw several waterfalls on the walls. Facing him was the throne seat and within it was Bantos. A chuckle muffled from his mouth as he rose up and applauded the Lithonian for his arrival.

"I knew it wouldn't take you long to defeat Roht. He was a tough warrior in my ranks. However, I've always known his skill could be outwitted by someone of a much quicker speed."

"Roht was not in my sights to kill. I had to take him out to get to you. You're the reason I'm here this night."

"Well then, savage one. Here I am and a sword I hold in my hand. The question is, will you strike me down before I do the same to you?"

"One of us will meet our god this day and I believe it will be you."

"Let's make it so." Bantos grinned.

Bantos swung with a right swing of his sword, clashing the steel against Praxus' own sword. A smile grew on the Lithonian's face as he shoved off Bantos' sword and sliced down toward the Bandorian's abdomen. Stepping back to look, Praxus let out a quick scoff.

"Are you worried? All men bleed."

"You forget, Lithonian. I am not all men." Bantos glared. "I am above all men!"

"Best to show it than to speak it."

The two clashed their blades once more with a more forceful push from Bantos, stumbling Praxus toward one of the waterfalls. The sound of the flowing waters increased in Praxus' ears as Bantos continued to push him closer. Bantos turned his gaze toward the waterfall and back to Praxus. A thought entered his mind as he let go of Praxus and kicked him into the waterfall. Praxus rose up as the water fell onto him. Stepping forward, Bantos rushed in and grabbed the Lithonian by his neck, holding him down in the water.

"Let's see how long you can live without a moment's breath." Bantos laughed.

Praxus struggled against the might of Bantos. For a man who appeared to be nearly of old age, his strength was of a young man. A peculiar trait in Bandoria. Praxus pushed with his chest, raising up from the water to Bantos' dismay. However, Bantos pressed his boot atop the back of Praxus, shoving him back into the water.

"Just give up." Bantos chuckled. "Accept this death and wander the afterlife with pondering questions of an alternative."

Praxus screamed as the bubbles rose to the surface. With enough strength in him, Praxus shoved off Bantos and arose from the water. His arms stretched and his fists gripped.

"What?" Bantos questioned with fear. "Such strength from a Lithonian is not possible. It is not."

He turned to face Bantos as the Bandorian king went to retrieve his sword from the floor. It was not quick enough as Praxus lunged onto him and pummeled his face in with punches. Praxus continued the blows even as Bantos attempted to block them with his arms and hands. Praxus stood up and kicked Bantos in the chest. Turning back, Praxus went and grabbed his sword and raised it above the neck of Bantos.

"If this is my end, let it be a quick one." Bantos said.

"Otherwise, you'll end up dead sooner than I."

"Enough. Your end has come."

Praxus rose up his sword for the kill and setting to make their mark, seven Bandorian soldiers bolted into the throne room with sword sin hand. Without hesitation, they saw their king on the floor and Praxus standing over him with his sword near his neck. The soldiers screamed as they attacked the Lithonian to save their king. Praxus fought back against the soldiers, swinging his sword to their own surprise. The Bandorian soldiers are used to their enemies quickly submitting when there's more than four. However, such was not possible with Praxus. For his is a Lithonian and Lithonians do not fear numbers. They do not fear anything aside from their own failures and dismays. Praxus gripped the hilt of the sword and impaled one soldier into another. Pressing their bodies against the wall as they fell into one of the waterfalls. Turning to the remaining five, Praxus moved with speed, hacking and slashing his blade against their thighs and forearms. It was within a matter of minutes in which Praxus had slaughtered the soldiers. Their bodies lying on the clear marble floor with the blood pouring through like spilled wine.

"Now to finish you off." Praxus said, turning around to face Bantos.

Bantos was gone. No longer was he lying on the floor within his throne room. Praxus turned around and searched the room with haste. No sign of Bantos caused a yell to echo from Praxus. Sounding off throughout the palace and reaching the peek of the city. Even Brithon and his soldiers heard the roar of the Lithonian.

"I wonder if he accomplished the goal." Brithon said to himself.

Praxus looked at the dead soldiers around him as he could hear the running footsteps of more soldiers incoming. Taking the moment to see the throne seat, Praxus carved a mark into the seat as he made his escape just in time before the soldiers arrived. While the soldiers signaled the city to search for the Lithonian, Praxus had returned to the outside where he was greeted by Brithon and his soldiers.

"Did you do it?" Brithon asked.

"I was close. His men were onto me before I could take the strike."

"So, he still lives."

"Yes. But, not for long. He's wounded."

Hearing the bell sounding as the noise of the rustling civilians began to scream, Praxus and Brithon took their leave. Returning to Brithrow. It was only a matter of days when Bantos sent out the decree for all his soldiers to find Praxus and to bring him to the palace for his sentence. A sentence which would only be death under Bantos' rule. Praxus was informed of the decree by several of his Lithonian spies.

"If he wants me, he'll have to find me." Praxus said. "Or, when I find him."

Elsewhere in the far regions of the land, word had spread of a familiar, yet mysterious weapon was discovered near the hills of the Megarian Mountains. Praxus heard the news and grinned with pleasure. Speaking to his Lithonian brethren, Praxus had set out to uncover this mysterious weapon and plotted to use it against Bantos to bring a full end to his tyranny. Praxus had spoken with Brithon concerning the quest as Brithon had begun to warn him of the dangers which rests near the Megarian Mountains. Threats from giant beasts, savage dwellers, mercenaries seeking challengers, and even the legendary Valley of the Lost. All would bring fear upon a normal man, yet, Praxus of Lithonia was not an ordinary man. He is a man of strength, speed, and valor. Loyal to his cause and to his people and allies.

Praxus had prepared himself for the journey as he gathered his equipment and sharpened his sword. Hearing of more powerful threats which may challenge him only gave him the excitement of a fight. The words of Dakin Maul still lingered in his mind. Their meeting was soon to come if the sorcerer's words were deemed true. That is only something Praxus can ponder on until the time comes. The following morning, Praxus had rode out of the Kingdom of Brithrow and set his travels for the Megarian Mountains. His true journey had just begun.

EXCERPTS FROM MARK PORTER OF ARGORON

CHAPTER 1: THE INCIDENT

United States Army Lieutenant, Mark Porter is currently on a mission to Roswell, New Mexico. His focus is keen as he traveled alone, listening to musical instrumentals. As he drove, his cell phone rings and he answers it.

"Lieutenant Porter." he said.

"Porter, this is General Dunlap." the caller said. "How far are you from the site?"

"I'm looking at it as we speak." Porter said.

Porter drove to the entrance gate, where two soldiers stood. They opened the gate , permitting him entry. Porter recognized the location, while still speaking with the General on the phone.

"General, I must ask, what is this place?"

"This is Area 51."

"Area 51." Porter intrigued. "I never thought I would be here."

"See you inside, Porter."

Porter hung up the phone, entering into the front entrance of the buildings. Area 51 had the appearance of a small city, with dozens of soldiers and officials moving throughout. Most of which are military soldiers and scientists. Porter stepped out of the car, heading towards the front doors layered with bulletproof glass. He entered, being greeted by soldiers. Porter took a left turn toward the elevator. Inside the elevator were two scientists.

"Excuse me, but are you Mark Porter?" one scientist asked.

"Yes I am."

"Its an honor to meet such a well-known Lieutenant." the other scientist said.

"Thank you."

The elevator had reached its destination floor. Porter is the first one to walk out, only to avoid the two scientists. Porter walked down a hallway and in the distance, he saw General Dunlap. Porter begins walking toward him. General Dunlap saw Porter coming down the hall near him.

"Porter, right on schedule."

"Yes sir, General."

Porter and General Dunlap entered another room. As they walked, Dunlap began telling Porter a few details to the secret operations being held within the facility. Porter took a guess to what it may be with only Dunlap smirking without saying a word.

"Porter, there are some rules that you must obey, since you're here."

"Ok, General. What are they?"

"You must not tell a single soul what you're about to see in this next room." Dunlap said. "If you do, we will have no choice but to rid you of the world."

"I see. Must be something very important."

"Important?" Dunlap said. "Try highly secretive. If anyone found out about this, the world will turn for the worst."

They reached the room and the metal door slowly slides open. The room was surrounded with military security. Little light was emitted into the room as the rest was covered in darkness. Porter gazed around, seeing scientists doing autopsies on unknown beings.

"General, what is going on here?" Porter asked.

"I'll tell you once we've reached our location."

Passing through the security, walking into yet another room. This room was lit up with plenty of light and wasn't nearly as shrouded in darkness like the other. Inside the room is a long table with a device sitting in the middle. Porter and Dunlap approached the table, looking at the device.

"Porter, this device you see here is able to transfer beings, human or not, to other worlds."

"Other worlds? Like planets?"

"Yes. Perhaps even dimensions are a possibility. Testing will only reveal how soon."

"How is that possible?" Porter asked. "Has it been tested?"

"Not yet. We're still awaiting an answer from the President."

They walked around the table, looking from all angles. The device was shiny, projecting a blue light which directed into the air. Porter slowly held his hand over the device before Dunlap snatched it from getting closer.

"You don't want to do something that you'll regret."

"Sorry, sir."

As they stood looking at the device, an alarm goes off. Porter and Dunlap look around. Dunlap ran toward the doors, questioning the security as to what triggered the alarm.

"What the hell's going on?!" Dunlap yelled.

"The base, sir, its under attack!" a soldier yelled.

"Porter, stay where you are!"

He pulled out his pistol, looking outside the door. From the outside, he saw soldiers and scientists being attacked by an unknown force. The opposing force appeared to have tentacles, while wearing peculiar white robes with long white hair extending to their lower back. Dunlap glared out of the glass window of the door, staring at them, watching them kill the soldiers and scientists. Gunshots are heard from the outside, but they're dying left and right.

Porter approached toward the door, but is stopped by Dunlap, who commanded Porter to stay by the table.

"General, what's going on?!"

"Sit tight, Lieutenant!" Dunlap said. "We're in for a show."

Dunlap backed from the door as it bursts open. He began shooting at the beings, but the gunshots have no effect. Porter takes out his revolver and shoots one of the beings in the head, which kills it. Dunlap looks at Porter, astounded.

"Try that, General."

"I surely will."

They both begin shooting the beings that are coming into the room through the damaged door. They aim for the head and shoot them directly there. They've killed the beings and look at each other. Both astounded and calm.

"Good job, Lieutenant."

"Same to you, General."

They shook hands, but from the ceiling a bright light shines down on them and Porter pushes Dunlap out of the way and a loud bang is heard with a large flash of light, nearly blinding Dunlap. The light fades away and Dunlap looks around for Porter.

"Porter?" Dunlap spoke. "Porter?!"

Dunlap looks around and realizes that Porter is nowhere in sight, but he also realized that the device's light is now dim, which before it was bright. He now knows that someone has happened to Porter.

Porter, who's opening his eyes, realizes that he's in a desert. He looks and stands up, brushing the dirt off of his uniform. He walks around the area, looking around at it surroundings.

"Where the hell am I?"

CHAPTER 2: CAPTIVE FOREIGNER

He continued walking, although realizing that he can move faster and jump higher than usual. Knowing now something isn't quite right. He continued to move ahead, but in front of him, he sees something running towards him. He tries to get a closer look and he sees that they looked human. He begins running the other direction, but is shot down by a bow and arrow. Porter lays on the ground as the beings get closer to him. He now hears silence, but the beings are surrounding him.

The beings appeared to be humans, yet there was a difference to them. Their skin was darker and their bodies were toned. They stared down Porter as he glared at them. They spoke to each other in an unknown language that Porter couldn't understand. He stood up, staggering from the arrow wound, stepping back from the beings and points to the one wearing white fur over his shoulders. His stature gave Porter to belief to be the general.

"You, where am I? Tell me where the hell I am?!"

The humanoids looked at Porter, their thoughts ponder if he's not from their world. One approached Porter and looks at him from all angles and stands back with his group. Porter stares at the group, reaching for his revolver, but he doesn't have it. He looks at what he perceived to be the humanoids' general and saw he had his revolver.

"How did you get that?!" Porter asked with rage. "Where am I?!"

Porter walked over to the beings, but he's knocked unconscious by one of their punches. They dragged him back to their location, locking him up. Hours later, Porter awakens and is now chained to a rock with no way out. He sees the beings from before, but this time, there's more. Porter begins thinking that he may not be on Earth anymore. He know believes that he's somewhere else, somewhere unknown.

Porter tried to break himself out of the chains, but he's too tired and weary to do so. He looks around as he's surrounded by dirt and feces. He continues to look around to find an object that could break him out of the chains. He doesn't find any tools that he could use, so he sits in the dungeon through the entire night. The next day, he awakens and sees himself surrounded by the tall, green beings. One in particular, releases him of the chains and helps him up, Porter stares at the being and looks into its eyes.

"What are you?" Porter asked.

"We are the Micrans." The being said. "Warriors of Argoron."

"What…? Argoron? Where am I?"

"You are on Argoron, stranger."

"Argoron?' Porter said. 'Where is that? I've never heard of Argoron.'

"If you're not from here, then, where do you come from?.' The being said. "What is your origin?"

"I'm not understanding what you mean? Where exactly am I?"

"You're on Argoron. A planet in the vastness of the stars."

"Argoron?" Porter questioned. "No. I was just in New Mexico."

"Where do you come from? Truly?"

"My name is Mark Porter." Porter said. "."

From the entrance came the leader of this particular warrior clan, Saban Jai. Saban walked toward and stood in front of Porter. Porter stared, not knowing what to expect.

"Mark Porter." Saban said. "How can you be from Jagoron?"

"What? No, I'm from Earth, not Jagoron? What is a Jagoron?"

"That is what I said, Mark Porter of Jagoron The world you come from is called Jagoron in this land. To your species, the earth-walkers, Jagoron is called Earth."

Porter sat confused. The Micrans didn't know what to make of his reaction. Saban didn't bother with him, rallying the others to bring him to the carriage. The carriage seemed to be made of a reddish wood as were the wheels, decorated with spears and red flags with no markings. Two of the Micrans carried Porter into the carriage, which was pulled by two eight-legged creatures. Which Porter saw them, he immediately thought them to be horses. However, he spotted they each had two tails and two sets of eyes on both sides. Speaking the word, Saban chuckled.

"Moreks." Saban said. "That's what they are. The fastest beasts in all of Argoron."

Saban jumped into the front of the carriage, gaining control over the horses as they rode off from the vast desert toward the massive metropolitan city as they approached the gates of the city of *Taranopolis*, as the inhabitants called it. Porter took a look outside of the carriage, seeing the massive city with its pointed skyscrapers and layered structures. The vehicles which moved throughout the city were a mix of the carriage and anti-gravity ships. The ships appeared to have four sets of transparent wings in the colors of rubies. The sky above the city was orange with a hint of red. The city was surrounded by red flags, flowing calmly with the wind throughout the city as the temperature was warm enough to have the people dressed in light clothing. Some even glanced at Porter, seeing his attire. From there, Porter knew he was out of place, especially when glancing upward toward the ships.

"Where am I?" Porter asked himself.

The carriage stopped in front of the city's palace. The Micrans stood by the carriage door, dragging Porter to the outside as they entered the palace. Porter stood on his feet, being held by two Micran soldiers, walking toward what he guessed was the throne room. In the room, Porter saw three chairs. Two were empty and the center one was full as there was a man sitting, speaking with another man. The man standing up had the wings of a dragon folded on his back and claws for fingers. Dressed in armored leather. The man sitting down was decked in armor, linen, and fur. On his head sat a crown made of what appeared to be gold or bronze. Porter couldn't make out any of it, yet, he knew they were royalty in their own way.

"You know why I've come and visited you, my lord."

"Yes, I am aware of your need for warriors. As of right now, there aren't many who are at my disposal for combat."

"What of your prisoners? What use will you have for them other than wasting away behind cell doors?"

The one in the chair nodded, rubbing his chin.

"You have a point."

They looked toward the entrance, seeing the Micrans carrying Porter. The man standing pointed and his yellow eyes widen. The man in the seat stood up, glaring toward the Micran warriors and the prisoner they held.

"A new prisoner?"

"My lord." Saban said, kneeling. "We have another prisoner in need of interrogation."

The man stared at Porter, seeing his clothing and his tone. He was uncertain of Porter's ethnicity to his own and the others around him. He turned back to Saban, raising his hand, giving him the order to stand.

"And what has this man done and what is he wearing?"

"We're not sure, sire. He was dressed in this manner when we found him."

"And where did you find him?"

"Out in the wilderness. He appeared dazed. Confused you might say. He was speaking strangely, so we brought him here. To get more answers. If you request it, my king."

The King nodded.

"Very well. Take him to the room. Ivo will be there to get any answers we may need."

"And what of him after you received your answers?" The other man said.

"When the time comes, I will call to you, Wyvern King. Right now, best you return to your domain. Prepare your warriors for the entertainment of the masses."

"I will keep my eyes and ears open."

The Wyvern King's wings buckled as he nodded his head, walking toward the exit. The King looked back, seeing Saban and the warriors leading Porter into the interrogation room. He sighed as he sat down and from the entrance arrived a young woman, dressed in a silver dress and long reddish-orange hair. She bowed before the king and he smiled.

"My daughter. I see you've returned from your journey."

"I have, father. I also have some news regarding the people of the city."

"News? What kind of news?"

"The people are aware of the coming war with the Celedians."

"And how do they know this?"

"Some have described a strange man coming into the city, warning them of the war and giving them the choice to choose which side they're on."

"A speaker of war in my city." The King said. "I see I must find him. Or, perhaps Saban has already brought him in."

The Princess wasn't sure what her father had meant. He chuckled and stood up, walking toward his daughter.

"Let me handle the matters of war. You must prepare for a wedding. Saban is a good man and a future leader."

"I… I understand."

The King looked at his daughter as she let out a small smile.

"I have other matters to attend to. Make sure you keep yourself protected when you're out in the city."

"The guardsmen will stand by me."

"Good, my Arribel."

CHAPTER 3: WHO ARE YOU?

Porter struggled against the strength of the two Micrans as they chained his wrists to the wall before exiting. Porter stared quietly, hearing footsteps approaching the cell. The door had opened for Porter to glance at two other warriors and a peculiar following the middle. He stood about the height of Porter, but he was much older as his white hair could attest.

"Who are you?"

"What?" Porter said slowly.

"Who are you? What is your name?"

"My name is Mark Porter."

"Mark Porter." Ivo said. "Strange name. never heard of such a one. Tell me, Mark Porter, where are you from?"

"I'm not from here. So, that's a start."

"Your name tells me all I need to know. Why have you come here, Mark Porter? Are you a spy for the Celedians? The Ceruleanians? Orgons, perhaps?"

"What are you talking about? I'm not from this place. "

"Your physical tells the tale. You're a warrior."

"I'm a soldier. A lieutenant."

"Convenient." Ivo chuckled. "And you've come here for what purpose other than being a spy or an invader?"

"I am not an invader nor am I some kind of spy. I didn't come here on my own accord. It's hard to explain. Even for myself. The place I come from is Earth. Earth is my home."

"Earth? You speak of Jagoron, the blue world where the waters move across the grounds."

"I guess you can detail it as much."

"Who sent you here?"

"I don't know."

"Then, start with something for me to go along. To understand your plight."

Porter sighed, waving his hands slight in a non-caring manner, yet, Porter began to tell Ivo of the encounter in Area 51, the ambush, and the instant transportation. Ivo listened closely to every word Porter had spoken. Once Porter had come to the conclusion of his sudden appearance in the desert, Ivo ceased him.

"You were brought here."

"Yes. But, I'm not sure by what or how."

"What is it you truly desire at this moment?"

"To be out of these chains and to be sent back home."

Ivo chuckled.

"There will be a time for that. Getting you back home however, is a tricky obstacle. For if you do not know how you came to Argoron, how does it make sense for you to find your way back."

"I saw the ships you people have. They're far beyond what I've seen. Now, I can take one of them and fly it back to Earth. A safe passage to get home."

"Enough." Ivo said, silencing Porter. "Our customs are far different than your kind. For one to achieve the freedom which one craves, they must earn it and win it."

"Win it? I'm not understanding."

"Combat. A trial to test your strength. To learn your endurance. Mentally. Physically. Spiritually. Only then will we and yourself see the conclusion to the whole matter."

"Are you telling me I must fight to get home?"

"Yes."

Porter sighed. Hanging his head low. He thought for a moment if this was only a dream. A hallucination, yet, with the small pain he felt in his legs, he knew it was real. All of it.

"I'm sorry. But, I am not going to be treated as some sort of amusement to you and your people here. I demand to be sent home."

Ivo turned back and walked toward the cell door. He opened it before taking a look back at Porter. Measuring him with a gaze.

"Your freedom demands on your fighting spirit. I hope you have one."

Ivo exited the cell, calling over a Micran guard. Ivo signaled the guard to keep watch of Porter's cell for the remainder of the day and throughout the night. Several hours later, nightfall fell over Taranopolis and the city was sleep. The sky which as glowing red had become as dark with glares and glistens of a peculiar bluish hue. Porter sat inside his cell. Barely ate the food they delivered to him. He looked over toward the guard sitting at the door. With the faint light shining from the window above him, Porter caught the glimpse of a key. Believing the key to be the only way out of his cell. Porter made a move, but remembered his wrists were attached to chains embedded into the concrete wall.

"Hey." Porter whispered. "Hey."

The guard jolted a bit, no movement afterwards. Porter sighed as he looked around the cell for something. Anything to get the guard's attention. Porter thought and glanced over to his left, seeing the tray of food. His eyes moved from the tray to the guard. Porter swiped his foot, kicking the tray against the cell doors, rattling up the guard as he jumped up with a sword in hand. Porter saw the blade.

"What's going on in there?" The guard asked.

"Water." Porter said. " I need water."

"Water? Where do you see any water?"

"To drink. I need something to drink."

The guard sighed and walked off, leaving Porter waiting. Unsure of what he could've waited for, the guard had returned, holding a small flask in his hand. He opened the cell door and entered, putting the flask on the ground as he unlocked the cuff from Porter's right wrist from the chain. Porter sighed and paused, quickly snatching he flask and smashing it into the guard's face before kicking the guard in the throat and stomping on his head. The helmet which the guard had word was cracked on the side. Porter looked to the guard's hand, seeing the key. He grabbed it and unruffled his left wrist. Being free from the wall, Porter grabbed the chest plate and helmet of the guard. Taking the sword last as he made his escape from the cell. Porter moved through the corridors quietly, avoiding other guards and even those who were playing a game of *L'agh*. In the distance, Porter saw the moonlight peaking from a doorway. Porter reached the door and found himself staring at the outside toward the vast desert. He sighed, knowing if he wanted to escape, going back into the desert was his only option. Porter made his move and ran out into the desert with only Argoron's moon as his source of direction.

EXCERPTS FROM RAIDERS OF VANOK

CHAPTER 1: VANCE HARLAN

As astrologists and astronomers continued their research pertaining to other living beings throughout the universe, Vance Harlan, a man specialized in the scientific community of interstellar space proposed a plan. His plans to travel into the stars through a wormhole, hoping to come out into another galaxy filled with life. Vance pleaded his plans and works to many other scientists. All of whom rejected. Vance even went as far as to proceed with funding from his own ship to travel into space. Backers were not impressed. Stating Vance was living in a fantasyland hoping to collude with alien beings.

During one meeting with the Department of Defense, Vance entered the room, brushing his blonde hair before seeing it was cornered by guards. He nodded with cockiness as he was unimpressed by their sheer attempt of intimidation. Vance stepped forward, sitting down at the desk with four members of the Department.
"I see you have my files." Vance said, seeing an open folder. "Well, did you read it? Or glance through it?"
"Mr. Harlan, we went over your works. Every bit of it."
"Every bit. Including the footnotes regarding the amount of

energy needed to supply such a travel?"

The Officials sat still, and Vance nodded slowly.

"I guess you did. Now I'm impressed."

"What we decided is that we cannot give you the funding for such a proposal."

"Why not? You read the file. You saw the details of this kind of mission. You know it's possible."

"Yes. We do." The second official said. "However, events prior to this mission have reverted our attentions elsewhere."

"Elsewhere? Like what the oceans?"

"This talk of alien life has gotten the public too far into our affairs and we, don't like that fact."

"But, come on. It's aliens. An opportunity to speak with intelligent life outside of our own planet."

"We hear you."

"But?' Vance said with a quick sigh of breath.

"We're invested in or current public affairs. The funding must go there."

"I don't agree with this."

"Doesn't matter if you do or do not." The third official said. "The decision has been made regardless of your work."

Vance wiped his face and slanted his head. He clapped his hands, startling the officials and jolting the guards. Vance looked around at he guards, seeing their firearms slightly raised. He waved them off with a laugh.

"Even they get startled."

"Thank you for your time with us, Mr. Harlan. You may go."

"I do however have one question to ask you. Just one."

"What is it?" The first official said.

"What is the true reason you have denied me funding for this project?"

The first official sighed before gazing over to the other three.

The second official shook his head, staying silent. The third official fanned his hands in the air and didn't give an answer. The fourth official stared at Vance and turned to the first official. Giving him a nod. Vance's eyes moved back and forth between the for officials.

"So, is he going to tell me or are you? I'm confused right now with all this staring and waving."

"I will speak it for you." The fourth official said.

"Good." Vance replied. "That's good. Now, what is it?"

"There was an incident that occurred over a month ago in Nevada."

"Nevada. Ok. I'm still not getting at what you're trying to tell me."

"An incident of forceful attacks took place at Area 51. One of our lieutenants went missing in the light of fire after the base was ambushed. He was unable to be found and is still missing."

"I see. But, with all due respect, what does a missing lieutenant have to do with my project's funding?"

"The cause of the attack were those intelligent beings you're so amazed by. They ambushed the base and attacked our men. Killed many and one of our best lieutenants is nowhere to be found. Now, do you understand why we cannot permit this project to go forward? Because those things you desire to meet, they want us all dead and this world theirs."

"Well, maybe they were antagonistic aliens. I mean all aliens cannot be enemies, sir. That's just not possible."

"Either way. This project is not going forward. You may leave us now, Mr. Harlan. Return to your other work. It's proven useful for our country and your life."

Vance stood up from the desk, grabbing his file. He still continued speaking with the officials, pleading they give him the funding. The officials continued to refuse until the guards stepped down from their post and surrounded Vance. Fully realizing his current predicament, Vance nodded and chuckled before taking his leave. Vance had returned to his home and from here, he set for to find a way to get his project going without the funding from the Department. Working nonstop for months while living in the outskirts of Phoenix, Arizona looking for an opportunity, Vance had come into communication with a much-wealthy foreign billionaire. The billionaire did not give Vance his name or location, only that he was interested in Vance's work and handed him the funding he needed. The billionaire's only request was for Vance to return to Earth once he had come into contact with extraterrestrials and that he should bring back with him physical evidence of their existence. Vance agreed to the commands and went ahead with the project. From there, a starship was built under the eyes of his colleagues and associates. Vance kept the project's workings to himself to avoid scrutiny and possible arrest from the government.

"Ah." Vance said, gazing at the starship. "She is finished."

The starship sat inside one of the hangars Vance had acquired from the military due to his previous works. Everything was in place for the travel and Vance had decided to wait until one clear night had come to make his launch. A week had passed and there was no clear sky due to the amount of clouds and precipitations of rainfall. Vance was annoyed by the weather's behavior. As if it was acting aggressive toward him, trying to get him to quit his project. Vance didn't quit and after a long day of rain, the night had come and the sky was clear. Vance had gathered all his gear and placed it inside the starship. The hangar had opened and the starship had launched into the sky. Vance was astonished at the speed of the ship and the stars around him. Several minutes had passed before Vance found himself in space, glancing out of the window looking down at Earth. Using a map he had placed inside the ship to navigate his goings. He went ahead and traveled. Passing through a stream of asteroids, a flash of light peaked through them, gaining Vance's attention. He moved toward through the meters toward the moving light. Once he came closer, the light flashed with such brightness that it caused the ship to jolt and from there, Vance could feel himself being pulled into the light and the ship with him. Vance kept his eyes shut from the blinding white-then-blue-then-red light. In a short spot of chance, Vance took a peek and saw the light was in fact a wormhole. A smile had formed on his face as he and the ship were sucked in and the light was gone. As if it was nowhere to be found. Like it was never in the stream of asteroids.

Within seconds, the ship was forced out of the wormhole with such speed, the ship had crashed onto a planet. Vance was calm, yet angry of his ship's damage. Exiting the damaged ship, Vance looked around, realizing he could breathe in the air. He looked down, seeing soil and grass. He grabbed the dirt and looked closer. It appeared to be no different than the soil on Earth.

"Shit!" Vance said. "Crashed back down to Earth."

While sighing in anger, the sound of a rushing wave crashed behind him. Vance had turned, looking at what he cold tell was a shoreline and the waves were crashing in with such force the ground had not flooded. Confused, he took a glance up to the sky and noticed it was a strange color. Not like the blue sky of Earth, but a very light greenish sky mixed with a layer of blue.

"What the hell?"

Vance had turned around to find himself quickly surrounded by beings that appeared to be hybrids. They had the upper bodies of animals and lower bodies of humans. They held what Vance could perceived to be guns toward him as he held his arms up. Somewhat shaking in fear. Not from the guns. One of the hybrids that appeared to be a Leopard-Man stepped forward, measuring Vance. He nodded.

"Take him back to the ship!"
"Ship?!" Vance said. "What ship?!"

CHAPTER 2: WELCOME ABOARD

Tossed onto a ship decorated with skulls of various creatures. Creatures unknown to Vance's knowledge, the ship took off across the waters as the crew passed him by, operating the ship's movement. Vance sat confused. Mainly confused by the living hybrids passing him by. Standing up, he wandered around the ship, attempting to ask questions concerning where he is. Turning around as the sea's waters rush against the ship, tilting it back and forth, Vance approached an somewhat middle-aged man dressed in Captain's garbs.

"Pardon me, but, where am I?"

"Where are you? My good sir, you aren't aware of your current circumstances?"

"What circumstances must I be aware of?"

"We found you on that small island. Looked to me, you must've crashed from the sea above us. We found you stranded out here. Brought you onboard to keep you alive. You do want to remain alive, don't you?"

"Well, yes I do. But, I'm not understanding. Where am I?"

"Where were you going?"

"I was going through a wormhole and I fell back down. I must be somewhere around the Pacific Islands. I have to be."

"Pacific Islands? What is that?"

Vance paused, looking at the Captain with uncertainty. He

nodded while waving his hands, taking a gaze out toward the ocean.

"I'm still not understanding." The Captain said.

"We're on the Pacific Ocean, aren't we?"

"You're on the Sea of Aphro. The land around you is the Land of Aphro."

"Aphro?" Vance said. "What is Aphro?"

The Captain led Vance toward his study within the ship, passing by more hybrid creatures working. They enter the study with the first thing Vance noticed were the amount of scrolls laying on the shelves and the desk. The Captain approached his desk and opened a drawer, searching through, he grabbed a scroll and signaled Vance to approach the desk. Vance stepped forward as the Captain opened the scroll.

"What is this?" Vance asked.

"A map of this planet. Where we are right now is in the District of Aphro. Riding over the Seas of course."

"Planet? You said planet?"

"I did. Yes."

"Hold on. So, you're telling me, we're not on Earth?"

"Earth?" The Captain said confusingly. "What is Earth?"

"Earth. You know the third planet from the sun."

"Third planet? Third planet… Oh, you speak about Jarok. You're from Jarok?"

"Jarok? No. I'm from Earth."

"But, you said third from the sun."

"That is Earth."

"It is where you're from. Here, it's pronounced Jarok. Other words have been thrown out before. Depending on what planet you land on."

"So, if this is not Earth, then where am I?'

"Vanok."

"What is Vanok?"

"The second planet from the sun. second before Jarok and second after Firoh."

"Firoh? Jarok? I'm not understanding these terms completely. You mean Earth and Mercury?"

"If that's what they're called wherever you're from?" The Captain replied. "So, you are from Jarok. Tell me, how are things there? We never receive news regarding that planet. Only the other ones around it."

Vance took a moment to catch his breath. Taking all of the information in slowly. If possible. He glanced down at the map, seeing the landmarks. What Vance noticed quickly was the amount of water upon Vanok and the mid-to-small sized islands surrounding two larger continents. He pointed at the continents with questions. What were they and who dwelled upon them. Asking the Captain concerning the two continents. The Captain chuckled, using a cane to point toward the continents.

"The one we're nearby, Aphro. Of course. The other is Vetor. Now, there is a difference between the two."

"What kind of difference?"

"Well, for starters, Aphro is a continent filled with rugged structures and a plethora of diverse creatures. That's where my hybrid pirates come in."

"A whole continent filled with beasts."

"Yes. Now, Vetor. It's a much different place. Surrounded by beautiful landmarks and cathedrals. From tall skyscrapers to temples to the Vanokian gods. Vetor is the home of the Kingdom of Vetoria."

"And have you ever been there? To this kingdom?"

The Captain laughed, taking a breath before walking over toward his shelf, where a bottle of rum sat. Grabbing the bottle and taking a drink.

"Never. My kind, meaning my line of work isn't seen as acceptable in such a place. The people of the kingdom perceive myself and those like me as subservient. Lesser living beings. The kingdom believes they're above all life on Vanok. Even their own children to an extent."

Vance remained quiet as the Captain took a moment of silence. He sighed and returned to drinking the rum as the ship rocked. Strangely enough, Vance felt the movement of the ship a bit strange. The ship rocked once more with the sound of a bang following. He stood up from his seat, looking around.

"Did you hear that?"

"Hear what?" The Captain asked.

"The explosion. Something's happening."

"Let's find out."

The two run out to the front, seeing the pirates clashing against another set of pirates as the opposing ship crashed into their own. From the other ship jumped over pirates of a different kind. Wearing worn-and-torn clothing with a particular circular insignia layered on their chest. Vance kept his distance as the Captain yelled for his pirates to assemble and fight against the others. Vance watched on as the swords clashed and the gunfire rung. In the distance on the other ship, Vance spotted a figure making themselves known. Looking closer, he saw the figure in full form.

"A woman?"

The woman stepped onboard the Captain's ship and fought against several of his hybrid pirates with a cutlass of her own. She took them down in seconds as she made her way toward the Captain. Vance sought to help, grabbing a sword on the floor and rushing toward the woman. Seeing him from the corner of her eye, she turned with speed clashing her cutlass against Vance's sword. She glared into his eyes and showed a slight grin.

"You're different." She uttered. "This is the ship."

The woman signaled her pirates to grab Vance and they tossed him onto the other ship as the Captain looked on fighting against the invaders. Making the move to assist Vance, he was slashed in the back by one of the pirates before the woman rallied her own to return to their ship. They moved with motion, returning to the ship and they escaped the area. The Captain stood up, sighing in pain went around to check on his pirates. Seeing some of them dead on the deck, he sighed bitterly.

"Her." He whispered to himself.

CHAPTER 3: CALYPSO

Vance had sat on the deck of the opposing ship, surrounded by the invading pirates. Their eyes eluded him. Glowing in many glares of color. From black, brown, green, blue, and red. The pirates snarled at Vance, attempting to terrify him. Yet, Vance kept his composure and faced them. The pirates from that point had paused themselves and moved over to the edges of the ship, making way for their captain to step forward. She walked with a vigorous stature as her eyes were set only on Vance. She approached him and looked down onto him. A grin had formed on her face.

"What's going on?" Vance asked. "Why did you take me?"

"Poor one. You aren't aware of the workings here. I can sense you're not from this world."

"Of course not. I come from Earth. As I was telling the Captain on the ship."

"You mean the Captain of those degenerate pirates?! Ha! Such company will poison you. Eventually killing you."

"Then, why take me from them? I was seeming to be doing just fine. Doing well for the most part since I crashed on this planet. What is all of this and where are you taking me?"

"Hold your temper and follow me."

The pirates escorted Vance behind the woman into her study. Looking similar to the Captain's own, yet detailed with colorful marbled walls and a stone-layered floor. Vance saw the floor and took a look back out to the deck, looking at its wooden bottom. He had questions and the woman only replied with the notion of her ship's design was possible due to her line of work. Vance wondered what work she spoke of as she sat down at her desk, covered with books and maps. Even a small emerald sat on the desk in the right corner. Like a pedestal of her achievements.

"Leave us." She told her pirates.

Exiting the study, Vance stood in the center of the room with the woman signaling him to sit down. He went and faced her. Sitting down and staring while admiring her exquisite interior design work. Vance gave a nod. Impressed by her choice of style. She waved it off like a small gesture of good fortune.

"You may be wondering why I took you from those hybrids and why you're here."

"I am wondering? What was the reason. How come you're different than your crew?"

"Because they've learned to respect me."

"I guess you were just a woman looking to do something others refused?"

"Refused is a slight word to use in my line of work. No, they did not refuse, yet, they didn't survive the pathways."

"Survive?"

"Most of the people on this planet strive to live. It is a necessary evil one must do in order to obtain food, water, and supplies to maintain their lives. The majority on this planet have even scraps to survive. To make amends to their gods and to keep their families safe. The some, they only seek to acquire whatever it is they need and they're content. So they shall be. But, the few. Oh, the few. The few do what they must to survive. Even if they have to slaughter, make war, or enter conflict with the others. In the end, the few have always won. Vanok is their world and not the other way around."

Vance nodded slowly, taking in her words.

"And you happened to be one of the few?"

"I am now. Before I was one of the majority. My mother and father did what they could to give me a proper childhood. However, war had fallen and my father went into battle. He survived the conflict, of course. But, his health declined due to the weapons used in the war. Chemicals that have transferred the sky above into the warping it appears today. Afterwards, my mother took care of me until I was able to take care of myself. I learned as I traveled the two continents. Searching for new ways of work and opportunity. The majority had always preached to me that marriage was in my future. That I would find a man who I would be suitable to match. Funny, after all the men I've encountered, none of them saw me as wife potential."

"I'm sorry to hear that." Vance said slowly.

"Don't be. It taught me something important. As I learned the true nature of this world, I became one of the Some. Learning new things and new ways to make things work. I tried to tell those I knew in my past about these things and they refused. Saying, 'You can't live like that. It's too difficult to make such a path. The carving would be detrimental to one's own health.'. Crazy stuff they believe. Yet, that's what holds them down. Holds them back from increasing themselves. Elevating one's self is a sure way to make a move in this world."

"And what kind of carving did you make for yourself in this world?"

"First off, was military duty. I served in the Navy of the Kingdom of Vetoria. Fought countless battles on and off the seas. Most of my conflict was with the hybrids. We are taught in the forces the hybrids are responsible for more of the planet's dire circumstances. The increasing of the seas and the warping sky. All caused by their existence. The Navy's task was to eliminate any hybrids we encountered. And so we did."

"So, now you lead a group of pirates to do what exactly? Hold on. Is that why you ambushed the ship and took me?"

"Yes and no. Yes as in I ambushed the ship because they were hybrids. It's in my nature now. And no. I did not attack them simply to take you. Well, I didn't know you were onboard to start with. My intentions were simply elsewhere. That is until I saw you myself. From that point I had to take you."

"But why?"

"You're not a Vanokian. That much is true. Your essence oozes off your body. Your spirit's scent emits from you like a foreign soul."

"You know I'm not from this planet then."

"Certainly. What I want to know is why did you come here? What attracted you to Vanok in the first place?"

"First off, I didn't even know there was a Vanok to begin with. I was simply traveling through a wormhole and I ended up here. That is what happened."

"Truly?"

"Yes. Otherwise I would've had directions to go. I had no directions other than a wormhole."

"You said you're from Earth." The woman said, leaning in her chair. "Tell me, what is this Earth you speak of?"

"As I told the Captain of the Hybrids, Earth is the third planet from the sun. Second to Venus and first to Mars."

"I've never heard of Earth or Venus or Mars. They sound interesting though. That I'll give to you."

"I must be in a whole different solar system."

The woman reached down and picked up a map, she laid it out on the desk and slid it closer to Vance. He leaned over and looked. It was a map of a solar system. Yet not the one he is knowledgeable of. The planets on the map were bigger and the stars were brighter. Even it's sun was more of a darker fireball than the sun he knew.

"From what you're telling me, you most certainly are. Listen, this is what this system offers you. The first planet from the sun is what we like to call Firoh, a fiery planet. Its air will consume anything it touches. Second is Vanok, where we sit this day. A planet covered in much water and less land. Third is Jarok. A mysterious planet. We often wonder if there is life on it at all. Besides that, the tech capable of interstellar flight is kept in the secret chambers of the King of Vetoria. Fourth is what we call Arton, a planet covered in red dust. We speculate no life has been on that planet for millenniums. Fifth is Zutah, the planet of the Eye. Not sure what that means. Scholars here are still speculating. Sixth is Tharnog, surrounded with debris it gives off a bright light the father you're from it. You can slightly see it during the nights. Seven is Ocenia. Called that because it is known to be a planet of only water. No land."

"But, how are you certain of this? Of all of this?"

"Because of the scholars. They keep the records of the history of the system. The books have been around for ages."

Vance nodded, wiping the sweat from his forehead.

"This is a lot to take in."

"It has that affect on newcomers. But, don't you fret, there's still a lot more to learn."

"I see."

"Now, back to what I was saying. Oh, yeah. Now. The eighth planet is called Poston, somewhat similar to Oceania in appearance. However, instead of roaring waters, suffocating mists."

"I'm not certain as to how that works."

"You breath it in, you die. Simple as that."

Vance looked at the map again, seeing two remaining planets. The one after Poston was smaller and white as snow. The planet after was as dark as coal. the two planets seemed to mirror each other, according to Vance's understanding. The woman noticed his interest in the two planets as she smiled and tossing back her long wavy hair.

"Those two are enigmas of their own."

"And why is that?"

"The one before is called Hailon, a planet covered in dense snow. Often times, the scholars believe its pouring snow every second of a day. Can you imagine, nonstop snowfall for the rest of your days?"

"No I cannot. Where I live, snow is a rare occasion. Often appearances. But, rare."

"You're saying it doesn't snow on Earth?"

"No. It snows. Yes. But, not everywhere gets it. Only portions receive it. If you understand what I'm trying to say."

"I hear you."

"Does it snow here? In these waters?"

"Several times during the Sapphire Cycle. But, that's a whole 'nother tale."

"And what of the last planet? It looks a bit eerie."

"Because it is. We call that one simply Abyssian."

"Abyssian?" Vance said. "Like the abyss?"

"Why else name it after."

The woman sighed as she glanced over to a clock which sat against the ship walls. Seeing the time, she stood up and called for her pirates to return. Entering the study, they surround Vance and hold him up as he begins asking more questions concerning his fate. The woman laughed as she approached him closely.

"At least tell me what you want from me?"

"Oh. I want nothing from you. But, I know someone who will."

"I'm not understanding."

"We're on our way to the Kingdom of Vetoria. The King will like to have a word with you."

"The King?" Vance asked. "Why me?"

"Because you're the first being to come from another planet in ages. Such an event is one the King would not like to miss."

"Hold on. How does he know I'm here?"

"We have our ways of contact. Remember me saying something about tech earlier. It works in many ways. Ways the Majority will never come to understand and the Some refuse to use in order to advance themselves."

The woman commanded the pirates to take Vance to the guest room on the ship. Dragging him down the hallway, they opened the door and tossed Vance inside. Shutting the door before he could make a turn-around. Vance looked at the room, seeing a bed, a dining table, and a shelf of books. He looked over toward the shelf, looking at the books' spines, reading the titles. They were a mystery to him. All spoke about constellations and mysticism. Something Vance is not of interest in. While he were searching through, a knock came from the door, startling him. He stood up from his knees and called out tot eh visitor. The door had opened and it was the woman. Closing the door behind her as Vance stood confused.

"Why are you putting me in here?"

"To give you some comfort before you meet the King."

"None of this is making sense."

"I can't treat you like a slave and bring you to the King. He'll see the way you were treated and make a conclusion from that point. He has ways which are peculiar to foreigners."

Vance nodded while sitting down at the dining table. The woman looked and nodded. Something came to her attention. She called her hands, startling Vance as she laughed. He shook his head, trying to keep his composure and mental state. This is a day he never expected to live. But, here he is.

"Very well. I'll have some food brought to you and you can take a moment to rest before you meet the King."

"Well, thank you for your sudden hospitality. Could've doe this earlier and I may have taken you differently."

"The day is not over and I am not easy to comprehend. Nor are my motives."

The woman turned to exit the room, but Vance called out to her. Catching himself before even thinking of what to say next. She stood still, waiting for Vance to speak. He nodded and had a thought. A simple one.

"You never told me your name? That is if you have one."

"My name." she said. "You want to know my name?"

"I would like to. Otherwise, I would have to refer to you as the woman who took me from the ship or the Invader."

"As much as I would prefer those two, I'll tell you my name. although, I must warn you. Not even my crew knows of my name and for your sake, I would like to keep it that way."

"Wait, how do they not your name? so, they simply call you Captain?"

"Captain is enough for them to know who I am and my worth."

Vance nodded in agreement. He understood her intentions for once. The woman took a breath before uttering another word. Something which took Vance off his guard. Seeing a slightly vulnerable state from the woman who invaded another's ship and fought off the hybrids before taking him.

"Calypso is my name."

"Calypso." Vance said. "Sounds, a little frightening."

"As it should be."

Calypso turned and left the room, leaving Vance in a frozen state of worry and insight. Vance sighed as he could hear the waves moving across the seas.

PRAXUS, KING BANTOS, KING BRITHON, AND MANY MORE CHARACTERS WILL RETURN IN:

THE SWORD OF PRAXUS

ABOUT THE AUTHOR

Ty'Ron W. C. Robinson II is the author of several works of fiction. Including the *Dark Titan Universe Saga*, *The Haunted City Saga*, EverWar Universe, Symbolum Venatores, Frightened!, Instincts, and others. More information pertaining to the author and stories can be found at darktitanentertainment.com.

Twitter: @TyronRobinsonII

Twitter: @DarkTitan_
Instagram: @darktitanentertainment
Facebook: @DarkTitanEnt
Pinterest: @darktitanentertainment
YouTube: Dark Titan Entertainment

www.ingramcontent.com/pod-product-compliance
Lightning Source LLC
LaVergne TN
LVHW030344070526
838199LV00067B/6446